Charles W. Brickell

Rosetta

A poem of the Southern rebellion

Charles W. Brickell

Rosetta
A poem of the Southern rebellion

ISBN/EAN: 9783337212988

Printed in Europe, USA, Canada, Australia, Japan

Cover: Foto ©Andreas Hilbeck / pixelio.de

More available books at **www.hansebooks.com**

⇀·ROSETTA.↽

A Poem of the Southern Rebellion.

BY CHAS. M. BRICKELL.

NASHVILLE, TENN.:
SOUTHERN METHODIST PUBLISHING HOUSE.
PRINTED FOR THE AUTHOR.
1882.

Preface.

WHEN the shafts of envious criticism were hurled against Byron's genius, he had the courage to exclaim, "Prepare for rhyme; I'll publish, right or wrong!" And under the same circumstances, I would not hesitate to make the same statement. But I have not written this for the purpose of challenging criticism. I know that it is imperfect in a great many respects; and with all of its imperfections plainly before me, I throw it upon the great sea of public opinion, asking the reader to regard it as the production of a boy, and nothing more. I have friends who will give it their support; and if it finds its way into the Southern household, and gladdens any heart, the purpose for which I have written will have been accomplished.

CHAS. W. BRICKELL.

Poplar Grove, Ark., Nov. 1, 1882.

Rosetta.

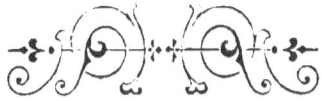

To Her

WHO HAS HONORED ME WITH FRIENDSHIP,

AND TO WHOM I AM INDEBTED FOR

KIND INSTRUCTION,

MISS SALLIE HARRIS,

OF FAYETTEVILLE, ARK.,

DEDICATE THIS LITTLE WORK AS A TRIBUTE

OF APPRECIATION AND RESPECT. .

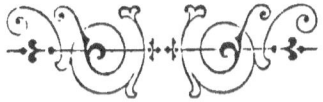

Chapter I.

O F that sweet land—"the Sunny South"—
  Where tunes the mocking-bird his mouth,
And ever lifts his notes of praise
All through the long, sweet summer days,
Together with the mingled song
Of other birds which floats along
The breath of eve so sweet and slow,
From mountain top to valley low;
Where nature with a willing hand
Sweet flowers scatters o'er the land,
Which ever lift their heads to greet
The angel tread and dainty feet

Of Southern girls: sing, muse—descend,
And all thy powers vouchsafe to lend
To me who will attempt in rhyme
To backward roll the tide of time.
Old Virgil in the classic days
Of Rome sung of her name and praise—
Sung of her heroes brave and bold
Who fought for empire and for gold,
And of proud Venus from above
Who gave Æneas Dido's love.
But I sing not as Virgil sung
Of heroes who were cast among
The angry billows, where they roar
Around the rocks from shore to shore,
And rugged coast whose turrets rise
Until they penetrate the skies;

Rosetta.

Nor rovers who wide oceans crossed
With vessels wrecked or tempest-tossed.
But hark! I now invoke the Nine
To lend their aid to my design,
And give a strain both loud and bold,
For I a story would unfold
Of love. 'T is of a boy, and girl
With smiling face and ebon curl,
And voice more charming far to him
Than music made by seraphim,
Or all the singing hosts above,
E'en if they sung of boyhood's love.
And he to her was dearer than
The living lordly race of man;
No matter what they might possess,
They ne'er could gain her sweet caress;

The right to kiss her smiling face,
And revel in her fond embrace,
Was held for him, because she knew
His heart to hers was ever true;
She knew within his breast alone
A heart pulsated to her own.
Since childhood's happy, golden day
Together they had joined in play,
And in the field and rustic grove
They each had told their childish love.
At first 't was only pledged in fun,
As through the meadows they would run
To chase the butterflies away
From roses in their childish play;
But as they both in years advanced,
And saw each other's love enhanced,

Their hearts, which had been joined in fun,
Now melted gently into one.
'T is love upon this sin-cursed earth
That gives our happiness its birth:
Without love, life a fraud would be,
Deprived of all felicity—
A shadow which we all would chase,
A long and toilsome weary race,
Where nothing would our gazes greet
That makes life now so pure and sweet.
The man that holds himself aloof
From woman's love and mild reproof
Had better died when he was young,
Or else when grown himself had hung.
The tale of woman's sins and fears
Comes gliding down the stream of years,

And all who read it quick believe
That God made woman to deceive.
They credit her with all the pain
The race has felt since Adam's reign
Was broken by the direful wrath
Of God, who put them in the path
Which led from Eden's holy way
To sin and death and sure decay.
Men loudly boast this feeble tale,
And say that woman 's weak and frail,
But man, who lords creation through,
Is strongest, bravest of the two,
And raise his name and virtue high,
And laud his praises to the sky.
Poor woman was they say the cause,
And one who first transgressed the laws

Of God, and brought us sin and woe,
And all the ills the heart can know.
Admitting that she broke the link
'Twixt God and us, stop, man, and think:
If all that tale of sin be true,
Old Adam ate those apples too;
And worse than that, stood forth and lied,
And thus his weakness strove to hide,
And trembling did this tale repeat:
"The woman ate, and made me eat."
Although she ate that sacred fruit,
And thus brought death to man and brute,
She never charged the man with blame
To save her honor and her name,
Nor tried herself of guilt to rid
By lying, as old Adam did.

But when she ate the apple sweet,
And Adam overcame complete,
She brought us Christ, whose blood was spilt,
A ransom to redeem her guilt.
I care not what we gained or lost,
Or what this woman's follies cost,
She ever bends us to her will,
And we revere and love her still.

Chapter II.

A SOUTHERN youth and Southern maid
  Were seated 'neath a rustic shade,
And while the stars shone from above,
They talked of pure, devoted love.
The moonbeams in a silver sheet
Threw shadow lace-work round their feet,
As falling gently through the trees
To kiss the silent evening breeze.
The golden sun long since had set,
But still they lingered, lingered yet;
For ere he said the night's farewell,
He needs to her a fact must tell.

2

She looked into his manly face,
And quick beheld the solemn trace
Of sadness, for he was distressed—
His heart and spirit seemed depressed.
She fondly gazed into his eye,
And said to him: "My darling, why
Do you this steady silence keep,
And to the charms of nature sleep?
Behold yon beaming stars divine,
See how they in their beauty shine,
And, thrown round all, the blue expanse,
Which seems their beauty to enhance.
And see yon regnant moon, so bright,
Fling forth her rays of royal light;
All nature now seems to rejoice,
But yet you hold a silent voice.

Dost thou not hear the whippoorwill
Pour forth his notes so loud and shrill,
And every insect lend its strains
To honor beauty where she reigns?
Ah! listen to the music made—
'T is nature's evening serenade."
He gazed into her rosy face,
And pressed her in a fond embrace,
Then left upon her cheek a kiss
(Now who will censure him for this?);
And then his sullen silence broke,
And unto her he calmly spoke:
"Rosetta, I have loved you long—
This passion has been true and strong;
And if I should remain with you,
Your heart to mine would still be true;

But if I should be called away,
For months and years perhaps to stay,
Where you not soon my face could see,
Say, would you still be true to me?"
She leaned upon his manly breast,
While he her raven locks caressed.
At last she raised her curly head,
And kissing him, she fondly said:
"Be true to you! how can you doubt?
I could not live a day without
Some thought of you, my model boy;
You are my hope, my life, my joy.
No matter where your lot be cast,
I loved you first, I'll love you last,
And true to you I'll ever be—
I only live to cherish thee."

"'T is well," he said, "I know your heart.
I need not tell you we must part—
How long 't will be I cannot know,
But all I have now bids me go;
And though to me 't will be a grief,
From it I shall find some relief—
Because I shall have this to keep
And kiss each night before I sleep."
As this he said a merry laugh
Escaped him, and a photograph
Of her he held before his face—
It seemed to smile with modest grace.
He looked into its face so fair,
And kissed it with a pleasure rare.
"You say that you must go away,"
She said, "for months and years to stay,

But still refrain from telling me
Why you should go and absent be.
Now do not longer wound my heart
By telling me that we must part,
And yet to me no reasons give,
But bid me stay, and hope, and live.
That you should go there is no shame
Of guilt upon your heart or name;
Then tell me, for I fain would know,
The reasons why you have to go."
"Tell you the reasons why?" he said,
And smoothed the ringlets of her head.
"Abe Lincoln loudly blows his blast,
The States are now seceding fast,
The war-dog with his bloody mouth
Is loosened on 'the Sunny South;'

The farm, the pulpit, and the bar,
Have each and all prepared for war,
And men are rising far and near,
To fight for that they hold more dear
Than life—our fair and 'sunny land'
From being crushed by Envy's hand.
The North to us its pledge has broke,
And forced upon our necks a yoke
Extremely cruel and unjust,
And one which crushes to the dust.
The North and South with all their might
Engage a long and bloody fight;
The South strives for her will and way,
The North for power and for sway,
And holds it true it should dictate
To every free-willed Southern State.

I never will withhold my arm
From striking those who do us harm;
But bravely will I stand and fight
The Vandals who on Southern right
Would tread—e'en though I wounded lie
Upon some field of blood to die.
Before this bloody war is done,
My bones may whiten in the sun;
But if by fate I should be spared
For those to whom I am endeared,
I swear, by yonder stars which burn
With light, I will one day return.
But if I am in battle slain,
And prostrate lie upon some plain,
Tell me that you no one will wed
Until you know that I am dead;

For if I should this war survive,
And both of us should chance to live,
I swear I will return to thee,
And claim that heart you pledged to me."
He gazed into the distant west,
And on a star his eyes did rest;
There seemed a smile upon its face,
As it rolled on through boundless space.
Why is it when man feels his love
The world beneath, the world above,
And every thing which meets his sight,
Fills him with feelings of delight;
The hill, the mountain, and the sky,
And every breeze which passes by,
Seems breathing in his pious soul
A love for nature's perfect whole.

If once you rob the human heart
Of love, you bid its joy depart,
And cast us on Destruction's stream,
And make our lives a foolish dream.
'T is love that fills the soul with joy
When ills and cares the heart annoy;
And God has placed it in the breast,
That man may be forever blest.
When sorrow wets the sparkling eye,
And trouble makes the heart to sigh,
Love calmly soothes the rising grief,
And bids us find in her relief.
To man it makes no difference where
Or what may be his station here,
He will an object early find
On which to feast his heart and mind.

And when to love he pays respect,
All nature wears a sweet aspect;
The dullest place in all the earth
Will to his mind give beauty birth.
And thus it was this lover stood
As if he was by nature wooed;
The earth, the sky, the breeze of night,
Seemed him to fill with sweet delight.
He stood and gazed in rapture there
Upon that single shining star,
As if the impulse of his soul
That orb held under its control.
At last he left the shining star
Which glittered in its home so far,
And turned his thoughts from realms above
Upon the lady of his love.

For she it was who held the sway,
And led him on from day to day—
The star to which he looked for light
To guide him in the path of right.
For who will e'er this truth dissent,
That woman is the element
That builds man up in faith and hope,
And cheers him up life's rugged slope?
She gives him will when he would sink,
And when he speaks she makes him think,
And in a thousand different ways
Compels his love and wins his praise.
If to be perfect man aspires,
Or to be great his soul desires,
What higher standard can he find
Than woman's pure and noble mind?

Search all your annals o'er and o'er,
And all the by-gone years explore,
Then in this vast and broad domain
Of time, which stretches like a chain
From Eden's fair and sunny clime,
Until it links the present time,
Show what more noble relic stands
Than that reared by a woman's hands.
The noblest man, the grandest name
That burns upon the scroll of fame,
Glows brighter still, and still more fair,
If woman helped to place it there.
Who then can wonder why this boy,
With admiration and with joy,
Viewed her, the spirit of his dreams,
With hope and pleasure's brightest gleams?

"I swore to you by yonder star,"
He said, "I would outlive this war,
And when I came would claim you then,
And we would never part again.
Now when the evening scarce from sight
Still lingers on the skirts of night,
And yonder shining orb you see,
I pray you then remember me.
To-morrow's sun shall scarcely rise
To gild the azure eastern skies,
Or herald forth the new-born day,
Before I shall pursue my way.
Rosetta, rise at early dawn,
When dew-drops sparkle on the lawn,
And long light shakes across the sky,
And we'll exchange a fond good-by."

She laid again her head to rest
Upon his young but manly breast;
He smoothed her black and waving hair,
And bid her discard every care.
The shining stars in silver shrouds
Concealed themselves behind the clouds;
And true the smiling queen of night
Behind a cloud shut off her light—
Would not intrude her shining face
Where lovers stood in fond embrace.

Chapter III.

THE morrow's sun, with beams unshorn
  By cloud or speck, called forth the morn,
Which lingered in a golden sheen
On tinted leaves and meadows green;
The shining dew-drops flashed the ray
Of rosy-tinted, blushing May
Ten thousand ways the grass upon,
Like diamonds sparkling in the sun;
The mocking-bird and warbling thrush
Sung sweet cadences from a bush
That filled the breezy breath of day
And made the gilded morning gay.

Ere yet the rosy, blushing morn
Herself with beauties did adorn,
Rosetta did in silence wait
To greet her lover at the gate.
While in the birth of morn she stood,
A horse came dashing down the road,
And sitting on his back, erect,
She saw the one she did expect.
No knight within the ages gone
E'er put a brazen armor on
And rode more proud or bold than he—
This youth of Southern chivalry;
No grander army e'er dismayed
A tyrant than the South displayed
When from her stolid sleep she rose,
Like some strong man, to strike her foes.

When Mars upheld his bloody hand,
How many from this "sunny land"
Lay stiff and cold upon the field
Before the South her flag would yield!
Grand Southern flag of red and white,
You waved o'er many a bloody fight,
And stood triumphant day by day,
Supported by "the boys in gray."
But then you fell—ah, cruel thought!—
And all your triumphs came to naught;
But no dishonor blots your name,
Nor did your fall bring you to shame;
For when you fell to wave no more
Above the battle's din and roar,
The South around you mourning stood,
For she had washed you in her blood;

And though our cause you could not save,
Nor o'er us as a nation wave,
Yet we have loved and held thee dear,
And for thy fall shed many a tear;
Within our hearts so true and brave
We've made for thee a hallowed grave
In which to sleep till thou canst greet
The realms of fame beyond defeat.
"Good morning, love; I come to tell
You I must go, and bid farewell
To all the charms which round me lie;
Away to war, perhaps to die
Where no kind face will o'er me bend
To watch where life and death contend.
Before the earth again shall run
Her circling orbit round the sun,

Before the moon with glowing light
Shall gild again the dews of night,
And shed her rays on wood and glen,
I'll be with Davis and his men.
I do not go to write my name
With blood upon the scroll of fame,
But go because my country calls
Me to her aid ere yet she falls.
Think not because I go away
My mind and heart shall from you stray.
When in the battle's fiercest strife,
Where smoke and murder both run rife,
I'll think of you, and day and night
That thought shall nerve my arm to fight.
On some hard field or bloody plain
I may be numbered with the slain;

But what is life to be o'erthrown
When Southern rights are trampled down?"
"Go, go!" she cried, "and lend your hand
To drive oppression from the land
Which reels beneath the sturdy stroke
Of war and North's oppressive yoke.
If you love me as you have said,
Be brave, and have no fear or dread;
And in the rear-rank never lag,
But fight close round the Southern flag;
And if the old flag chance to fall,
Torn from its place by shell and ball,
Rush where it lies—all death defy—
Grasp it again, and plant it high;
And let your war-cry ever be,
'The South, Jeff Davis, and Bob Lee!'"

" Were I disposed to hold my hand
From war, I'd go, since you command;
For when the foe you bid me fight,
I know the Southern cause is right.
That dear old flag of white and red,
Made sacred by the honored dead
And men who daily waste and give
Their blood and strength that it may live,
I'll hold above the battle's din,
E'en though I die, till it shall win;
And if I fall, of strength bereft,
While foes oppress me right and left,
I'll shout, e'en in the cannon's mouth,
'Jeff Davis and the Sunny South!'"
As this he said he drew quite near,
And whispered something in her ear.

It must have been of love, for she
Blushed with becoming modesty.
She upward raised her sparkling eye,
And seemed by that to make reply,
" Enough—your horse—away—ride on."
One loving kiss, and he was gone.
She watched him till the mountain's height
Completely shut him from her sight;
And then she looked, but looked in vain;
Then, turning, wandered home again.
All day for him her silent grief
In flowing tears found some relief,
Like clouds which mar the skies of day
" In showers weep themselves away." .
Then did the moon in glory rise,
While yet the sun in barren skies

Lay sinking, like gold-burnished ore,
Behind the vernal western shore.
While thus the sun and moon in lands
Far distant smote their golden hands,
Rosetta stole beneath a shade
Where Night her beauties had displayed;
And while the stars in beauty shone,
She watched the glintings of the moon.
"Ah, moon, why soarest thou so high
Across the trackless, star-lit sky?
To gild the daisies while they sleep?
Or watch young maidens when they weep?
Turn thou thy sight, O moon, away
From weeping maids and daisies gay,
And o'er my love with peerless light
Keep silent watch and ward to-night;

And when he sleeps beneath the sky,
Unguarded by the human eye,
O draw thou near, and guard him well,
Thou lovely watch and sentinel
Of night!   And if on rose or thorn
He sleeps, wake him, ere day is born,
By ringing blue-bells at his ear;
And he will wake if these he hear.
And when with beams of silver light
You gild again the dews of night,
While moonbeams play upon the deep,
Then kiss him in his peaceful sleep."
When she had spoken to the moon,
The old clock tolled the midnight noon
And in her moon-lit bower there
She breathed for him a tearful prayer.

Chapter IV.

'TWAS in eighteen and sixty-two—
"The boys in gray," "the boys in blue,"
Had met upon a battle-field
To test which side its arms would yield.
The golden sun hung like a ball
Of fire beneath the azure pall,
And spread his shining wings of gold
O'er turrets high and castles old,
Till nature blazed with burnished hue,
And made her rocks and mountains new.
All day the cannon's sullen roar
Had waked the echoes o'er and o'er,

And sent a deafening sound along
To chorus with the war god's song.
E'en while the battle madly waged,
And each their strongest force engaged,
The contest was so fierce and long,
And each side fought so brave and strong,
The sun stood still above the din
Of war, to see which side would win.
And then he sunk behind the west,
To pillow there his head in rest;
But as he sunk in western sky,
Ten thousand soldiers sunk to die.
They fought heroic, brave, and well,
And thousands of each number fell;
But ere the bloody work was done,
" The boys in gray " the field had won.

Upon that field of blood-bought fame—
Where gained the Southern boys a name,
Which will forever sound along
Time's corridors in Southern song—
A youth lay stretched upon the ground,
His life-blood flowing from a wound
He had received that fearful day
While fighting for that sacred "Gray."
His thick and auburn curly hair
Lay scattered o'er his forehead fair,
His face upturned lay to the sky;
And to the moon he breathed a sigh,
As she in regal beauty shone
Above the work that war had done,
And poured her peerless silver flood
Of light above this field of blood:

4

"Ah! dost thou, moon, in splendor rise
To light thy pathway through the skies?
Or dost thou soar so high above
To watch my bright-eyed lady love?
You cannot fail to know her, moon—
Her cheeks are like the rose of June,
And eyes as bright as yonder star
That glitters in its home so far;
Her voice, so sweet and pure and gay,
Is like the sounds which die away
Upon the waters—from a string
Of gold—when merry mermaids sing.
If such you see, while high you soar,
It is the one whom I adore;
Then tell her with a kiss for me
That she no more my face will see.

Tell her that now I wounded lie
Upon the battle-field to die;
But that I fought with all my might
Within the hottest of the fight,
And that I did no duty shun,
Nor fell until the field was won.
' The blue boys ' bravely fought, but fell
Before the Southern shot and shell,
Like mist of morn which fades away
Before the piercing god of day.
Tell her I saw our flag wave high,
I heard the Southern battle-cry,
"Sweet Sunny South," and with delight
Saw victory kiss the red and white.
Tell her that when my fleeting breath
Warned me to feel the touch of death—

Even while life's sands were falling fast—
I loved her fondly to the last."
The moon looked brightly from the sky,
And seemed to nod a sweet reply,
Then, smiling in his haggard face,
Rolled on through boundless fields of space.
A comrade in that battle wild
Bent o'er this wounded Southern child,
And smoothed his locks of curly hair
With soldier love and soldier care.
" Why speak you thus ? " he watching said,
" You will not die, nor yet are dead ;
Before the moon three times shall wane,
You 'll see your home and friends again ;
To-morrow's sun shall scarce be risen
From out his Oriental prison,

To light another new-born day,
Before you shall be on the way
To those you love." He held the hands
Of him struck down, and watched the sands
Of life move on, and knew with joy
That death claimed not this wounded boy.
With gentle hands he gently bound
And stanched the bleeding, ugly wound,
And did untiring vigil keep,
While Henry nursed his thoughts in sleep.
When ills and sickness evermore
With pain oppress the body sore,
Or downward press the heart with grief,
Dame Nature gives her sweet relief;
Sweet, balmy sleep—that placid stream
Where all may lose their cares in dream.

The prince, the peasant, and the poor,
Of every clime and every shore,
Have each a right to claim repose
In sleep, and rid themselves of woes.
The sleep of king is not more sweet
Than serfs who slumber at his feet;
Nor brighter dreams or visions sees
Than he who sleeps beneath the trees.
Rank nor position, place nor name,
Can e'er monopolize or claim
The whole of sleep.   For when bereft
Of all he had, old Adam left
The priceless thing to each and all—
'T was all he saved from out his fall.
Young Henry in his dreams that nigh
A vision saw, and with delight.

The form of her he fondly loved,
He thought, stood by with smile unmoved.
He gazed into her happy face,
And reached to get a kind embrace,
But quick she faded from his sight,
Like mist before the morning light.
'T is so with fortune: every day
We see her frisking by the way
Of life, but when to her draw nigh,
She shies around and passes by.
A foolish thing indeed 't will seem
To say that life is like a dream;
But life consists, as each must find,
In mere delusions of the mind.
We dream the dream of love to-day,
To-morrow see it fade away,

And leave the heart both cold and chill,
Without one animating thrill.
Now build we high the hall of fame,
And rear a statue to our name;
But ere the world through gilded doors
Walks on its tessellated floors,
And to our name gives pomp and sound,
The whole thing topples to the ground.
The dream of life, with prospect bright,
Allures the mind, enchants the sight;
We grasp—the substance fades in air,
Nor even leaves a shadow there.
From childhood on life's beaten track,   ·
Where memory ever turns us back,
We see on every hill and slope
The bones and ghost of some dead hope.

Where are the childish pleasures sweet
We chased on sportive boyish feet,
When we from morn to night would rove
O'er hill·by laughing brook and grove,
Where notes would float on every breeze
From dryads singing in the trees?
Alas! those childish joys have fled,
And every treasured hope is dead;
While through the dim and misty past
Those childish hopes which could not last
Are sounding, through the aisle of time,
And telling with a voice sublime
That every earthly hope and plan
Peculiar to the mind of man
Will fade like visions in a dream,
Or snow-drops on a rapid stream.

How foolish then for man to strive
To make his name and deeds survive
His death.   'T is but an idle aim
To be forever chasing fame;
'T is true she leads a merry race
To those who seek to see her face,
And lures them on from day to day
With prospects grand and colors gay,
And makes each road and pathway sweet
By strewing flowers round their feet;
But then the grand and gay of life
Form nothing but a two-edged knife,
Whose polished blade and bloody use
Lie hid beneath the folds of truce,
And traitor-like must soon detest
And stab the heart which loved it best.

When in the bough the mocking-bird,
The South's sweet songster's voice, was heard,
Ere yet the golden, blazing sun
Had ris'n his shining course to run,
Young Henry, who had left his home
And gone on fields of war to roam,
Now turned his weary footsteps round,
And started homeward to the ground
Endeared to him by many a trace
Of friendship, and a smiling face
Whose smiles to him had been a joy
And pleasure since he was a boy.
'T was then he learned to love this girl,
Her rosy cheek and flowing curl;
And too, beneath the rustic shade
Which fell athwart the grassy glade,

How oft had he in days gone by
Gazed in her girlish, sparkling eye,
And read the tale of love it told—
Which, told and told, had ne'er grown old,
But gave his heart the same delight
When spoken last as on the night
When all the world was lost in dreams,
And fairies sported on the streams,
He pointed to the world above
And swore to her his righteous love.
Now while these days he'd left behind
Through mem'ry rushed upon his mind,
A sense of joy his bosom filled,
And every chord of nature thrilled.
Ah! who has never felt as much
From memory's sweet and tender touch?

Sweet memory, regnant queen who sways
The scepter of departed days,
And ever keeps before our sight
The deeds of darkness and of light,
Thou art of earth the joy most dear
To those who love and labor here;
But then to him whose sinful heart
Is seared by crime in every part,
Thou ever wilt his life annoy,
And prove a curse instead of joy.
No one can e'er his punishment
From thee escape by mere consent;
For when the world is lost in sleep,
And silence broods profoundly deep,
Thou ever wilt the felon's knife
Hold up which drank the blood of life,

And make thy never-ceasing tones
Grate on his ear the victim's groans,
And show him in death's cold embrace
The wan and lifeless, pallid face.
But then to those whose lives are spent
In love, thou art an angel sent
To gather food from days behind,
Wherewith to feed the pious mind.
And it was thus with that poor boy—
He seemed to find a precious joy
In thinking of the dear old place
Where he had left that smiling face;
But as he to her home drew near,
So close that he her voice could hear,
So weary were his limbs that day,
He, wounded, fainted by the way.

Chapter V.

THE god of day had sunk to rest
   Amid a golden, burning west—
The traces of the light he shed
While erst the earth his beams o'erspread;
And while he then reposed in state
Beyond the golden sunset gate,
Within the sky that eve of June
The stars stood gazing at the moon;
And as she shed her tender love
In silver rays from high above,
Rosetta walked within the light
Thrown by this peerless queen of night
5

To earth. Amid this lovely scene
A giant oak, with foliage green,
And head proud-lifted, grand, sublime,
Stood gazing down the aisle of time.
She paused beneath this aged tree,
Which at a glance could ages see,
But had no tongue wherewith to tell
Its tale of time—grim sentinel.
'T was midnight's holy, solemn hour
When she stood 'neath this moon-lit bower,
And in the solemn silence there
She knelt and breathed to God a prayer,
" That he would guide the one away,
And to her send him home some day
A soldier-boy of high renown,
And on his forehead honor's crown."

She prayed with all the tender love
That could a girl's devotion prove,
While silence reigned calm and serene,
A benediction on the scene;
And while she prayed to God above
This prayer of faith, this prayer of love,
There mingled with her lovely tone
A human sigh, a human groan.
She quickly rose upon her feet,
Ere yet her prayer was half complete,
And looked across the dew-drenched lawn
Like some wild, startled woodland fawn.
While stood she gazing there in fear,
Again it smote upon her ear,
And though it seemed a death-like voice,
It made her girlish heart rejoice;

For in that painful, death-like groan
There seemed to her to be a tone
Which she had heard, and knew full well,
But when and where she could not tell.
There seems to hang about the mind
And heart and life of all mankind
Some mem'ries which will vaguely come
To us from out their secret home,
And tell us of some tone or face
Which we have known, but at what place
We cannot tell.   They always seem
Like some wild, fleeting, childish dream,
But bring to us a kind of joy
Which knows no pain, knows no alloy.
She bounded o'er the moon-lit ground
To where she heard the painful sound,

And, lying in the moonlight there,
She saw a face—'t was lovely, fair.
Although 't was haggard, pale, and worn,
And of its finer texture shorn,
It did a charm and grace reveal
Which pain could not nor would conceal.
Into that face upturned to sky
She gazed and gazed with steady eye,
Until a cry she could not keep
Roused him from out his stolid sleep.
"Ah! is it you?" he groaning said,
And, doubting, rubbed his curly head;
"Or is it but another dream,
In which your lovely face I seem
To see? A dream it cannot be.
I know your rosy cheeks I see,

For thou art standing closely near,
And I your angel voice can hear."
She bended o'er his prostrate frame,
And whispered in his ear her name,
"Rosetta," and with joy and bliss
She gave to him one precious kiss.
She raised him to his weary feet,
And said to him, with voice so sweet,
"Lean on this arm, which lives for thee,
And it a strong support shall be;
For in this hour 't will me behoove
To cling the closer to thy love."
Him to her father's house she led,
And showed him to a downy bed;
Then through the night's dead stillness there
She watched while he slept free from care;

And when the sun fresh from the east
Spread o'er the earth a golden feast
Of light, she lingered near his side,
And kissed his lips with jealous pride;
And 't was to her a constant joy
To nurse this wounded soldier-boy.
She soothed his many pains and cares,
And bathed his brow with loving tears.
What is there 'neath the world above
Can e'er excel a woman's love?
Or what within the hollow span
Of earth excels the love of man?
When man, oppressed by cares, cast down
By grief, when ev'ry hope has flown,
Or falls upon life's rugged hills,
Sweet woman whispers, "Peace," and stills

The tempest in his raging breast,
And gives him too his wonted rest,
And with her own strong hands will roll
The weight from off the human soul.
She nobly works with willing hands,
While man looks on and idly stands.
We see her soothing care and strife
In ev'ry avenue of life
When she can any means employ
Whereby to add to human joy,
And as an angel will adorn
Our homes, and make our lives a morn
From youth to age, where sparkling streams
Of love flow through our various dreams.
Could Heaven give a sweeter joy
Unto this wounded soldier-boy

Than placing him, while stricken, there
Beneath his love's protecting care,
Where he could see her fair, sweet face,
With rosy smile and angel grace,
Which wooed his senses day by day,
And charmed his pain and care away?
What can we find to quicker cure
The ill the soul can scarce endure,
Or charm away deceit and guile,
Than woman's fascinating smile?
There is a power hidden there .
Behind her smile, so lovely fair,
Man can't resist or disregard,
Strive how he may, strive he how hard.
When Henry lay distressed by pain,
And turned him o'er and o'er again,

Like some storm-ridden bark which braves
The fierce contending ocean waves,
Rosetta's smiling face and form
Were like sunshine with cloud and storm.
The lovely girl soon nursed him well
Of all the wounds by which he fell,
And many happy hours had they
Among the fields and flowers gay.
Sometimes they'd wander to a hill,
At whose broad base a rippling rill
Meandered on in cheerful glee
Through groves and meadows to the sea;
Then, turning to the vale below,
They'd watch the blossoms nod and blow
Along the brook where lilies teem,
And bending kiss the laughing stream.

One day, when they had wandered long
The valleys and the hills among,
They, wearied, sat them down to rest,
And watched two robins build a nest.
" We 'll build a home like that some day,
When I once more have gone away
To war, and then returned to thee,"
He said to her, quite modestly.
The words to her he did impart
Of leaving struck into her heart
Like some sharp dagger heated red,
And turning round, she quickly said,
"O do not say you go again !
I am afraid you will be slain."
And with the thought that he might die,
She softly soon began to cry.

"Rosetta, cease to spend your tears;
Of being slain I have no fears.
To-morrow morn I go away,
But only go two years to stay."
He raised her then upon her feet,
And left the grassy, cool retreat,
And wandered home, just as the stars
Sent forth their shining silver bars
Of lovely light, and day withdrew
For night to baptize earth with dew.

Chapter VI.

'TIS summer's eve; the golden rim
 Of sunset glows above the dim
Of distant clouds, now floating 'way
In lazy line at close of day.
The mocking-bird has hushed his song
Of joy and mirth, which all day long
Has floated on the scented breeze
From hill and vale to woodland trees,
And now sits in submissive mood;
For ev'ry sound has been subdued
In nature, if except we one
Which even now is floating on

In lovely strains—not fierce or wild,
Nor weak as if they from a child
Did come; but 't is a maid who sings,
And on the night's dead stillness rings
Her voice, so sweet, so pure and clear—
It is Rosetta's voice we hear.
Wooed by the night's enchanting hour,
She sits a victim to its power,
And with a voice not loud but strong
In pensive joy she sings this song:

I am sitting by my window to-night, love;
 Gems are setting in the sky;
The proud queen of night is smiling from above,
 As the stars she gayly passes by.

While the heavens are aglow with her peerless light,
 And the sparkling beams so free
Are falling from the gems in the crown of night,
 I am thinking, darling one, of thee.

'Tis sweet, O how sweet, to sit and fondly think
    Of the happy days of yore,
When beside the sparkling stream upon its brink,
    We would tell our young love o'er and o'er!

O how happy were we, sitting there alone!
    And to-night my heart would fain
To turn the tide of time, if such could be done,
    And live those sweet days o'er again.

But the blighting hand of war has cursed this land,
    And has cast our lives apart;
But we will meet again, because affection's band
    Closely binds mine to your loving heart.

But should fate so decree that we shall never meet,
    And us happiness deny,
I will oft steal at night to our sweet retreat,
    Where we 've sat in happy days gone by.

6

I'll sit and fondly wait; your footsteps drawing near
  Tell me your form is nigh,
Or your gay, merry laugh the breezes shall bear,
  As they frisking gayly pass me by.

When there I've waited long, O should you then not
  I will know I've lost your love;   [come,
That you are wrapped in death, and a happy home
  Have found with the shining ones above.

She sung this song now o'er and o'er,
As if her soul she did outpour;
For something in it made her feel
A strange delight she would reveal
That night, for 't was his time to come
Again unto his childhood's home.
And as she sweetly sung this song,
To greet him as he came along
The gravel-walk where often I
Have seen him walk in days gone by,

All nature hushed its noisy sound,
And listened in silence profound.
But as she sat and waited there,
Expecting soon his steps to hear,
His voice and footsteps sounded not
Upon the old, familiar spot,
But in his stead a letter came
Which bore to her his words and name.
The servant placed it in her hand,
And then withdrew, at her command.
She, doubting then 'twixt hopes and fears,
Upon it freely shed her tears;
Then tore it from its feeble case,
And through her blinding tears did trace
These lines :

    Rosetta, darling of my heart,
    'T is sad to think that we must part

Forever; but, my lovely one,
My race of time is almost done.
To-day we fought a fearful fight
From sunrise till the shades of night,
And when the sun sunk in the sky
Both friend and foe sunk down to die;
And even now my feeble breath
Tells me I'm wounded unto death;
But God is good, and high above
This earth I shall expect your love
To make me happy in that home
Where death and partings never come.
I feel, I know that I shall ne'er
Again your lovely accents hear,
That death our ev'ry hope will blast,
But still I love thee to the last;
And even now I fondly press
Unto my lips that lovely tress

Of curly hair I stole from thee
That night we stood beneath that tree,
When o'er the hill and brook and wood
The moon poured her bewitching flood,
And from the star-lit, azure sky
Smiled on my theft, then.passed us by.
Live thou in peace, sweet, gentle maid;
The hand of death cannot be staid
By any thing, not e'en by love;
Then meet me in the world above,
For ere these lines you shall have read
I will be sleeping with the dead.

Henry.

She gave one wild, despairing shriek,
As if her pure young heart would break;
Then prostrate fell she from her chair,
As if death's hand had touched her there.

She suffered—how much who can know
From this one awful, fearful blow.
Like some tall tree which cannot stand
Amid the storm by self-command
Erect, but ever shifts and bends
Before the rushing, driving winds,
Her spirit bent.   There is a grief
Which to my mind finds no relief—
A painless pang time cannot kill,
Nor make the waves of woe be still:
'Tis when the heart has fondly loved
Some object which has ever moved
The nobler parts.   Then cruel fate
With ruthless hand would soon or late,
Beholding that we loved it best,
Tear it from out the yearning breast,

And break each sweet vibrating string
By which the heart to it would cling.
The strong oak when its head is bowed
Before the northern wind and cloud .
Can, when the chilling wind and blast
And all the weather rough has passed,
Erect again hold up its form,
And show no scars from wind and storm;
The country o'er whose flow'ry land
Grim war has stretched its wretched hand
Can soon recover from its doom,
And then again in beauty bloom;
But when the heart is made to feel
The wounds which disappointments deal
In love, I think and say that none
From out the millions—no, not one—

Whose heart has e'er been made to move
In sweet response to mutual love
Can, when they feel misfortune's hand,
Again that sense of love command.
Let prudes and bigots all despise
The sweet impulses which arise;
But once when human love is hushed,
Man's better nature has been crushed.

Chapter VII.

TIME swiftly flew—the war had closed,
　The South once more in peace reposed,
But thousands of the brave who stood
Upon her fields dyed red with blood
Have never come to greet their place
Of birth and mother's fond embrace.
Brave boys they fell—brave, noble band—
Fell by the North's invading hand;
Gave to the evil powers of might
Their lives for that they knew was right.
Ah! many a mother heaved a sigh
As home-returning flanks went by,　　·

When looking o'er the list who came
She could not find her sweet boy's name !
And trusting then 'twixt hope and fear,
She would of those ask standing there,
" Can some one tell me when my son—
He went away in sixty-one—
Will be at home?"   Some one would say,
" In sixty-one he went away ?
Now let me see, perhaps I've known
This boy of yours; it was n't Tom Brown?"
" O yes it was ! pray tell me when
I 'll see my darling boy again."
"Your son? ah yes, I knew him well;
I've heard him round the camp-fire tell
His jokes and yarns, and tales of fun,
When weeks of marching had been done.

And then again we hand in hand
Have marched o'er fields of bloody sand,
And fought on plains of death and blood,
Where " blue " and " gray " alike have stood
The galling fire as brave as he
Who fought at Greece's mountain-key;
But ere the " bloody war " had passed,
Tom Brown, good soul, fell—shot at last—
Fell in my arms, shot through the head,
And when he spoke these words, was dead :
" Bill, " as he fell, he said to me,
" If mother's face you ever see,
Tell her Tom Brown her son is gone—
Died in the fight, his ' harness on ; '
That let the South be wrong or right,
I came to strive for her, and fight

For what I think is true and just;
And since I have to 'bite the dust,'
I'm proud I left my home and came
To die, e'en for the South's sweet name."
This told, that aged heart was wild
With grief, because she knew her child
Was gone.   Grim war had stuck its dart
Into a Southern, loving heart.
Among the ones who did not come
Again to greet their boyhood's home
At close of war was Henry; yet
Rosetta did not him forget,
But kept the field of memory green
With thoughts that he would come again.
When disappointment spreads its wings
Above the heart, and o'er it flings

Its dark'ning shades, there springs a love
Which all the pow'rs of earth can't move
To doubts and fears—joined with a hope
Which holds it, like the anchor's rope,
Securely bound and firmly tight
Amid the darkest storms of night.
And when Rosetta's heart grew weak,
'T was then this hope would to her speak,
And bring before her doubting gaze
The happy scenes of by-gone days,
When she and Henry all the day
Would chase the idle hours away.
Two years sped on, and still he staid.
Another lover to the maid
Poured forth his love in accent sweet,
And knelt beseeching at her feet.

He pressed his suit unto her long,
And sung to her full many a song
Of joy and love as hours flew by.
She unto him made this reply:
"No one I cannot, will not wed
Until I know my love is dead;
And then, if give him up I must,
I'll pour my tears upon his dust.
At morning and at close of day
I'll go my weary, lonely way,
And gather roses from the grove
Where first he pledged to me his love,
And with a heart both true and brave
I'll scatter them above his grave."
"He cannot come," this lover said;
"The war has closed, and he is dead,

Or else long since he would have come
To see again his friends and home.
Then why will you thus fling away
Your time and love in youth's bright day
Upon an object which to you
Is dead, if reason's tale be true?
No doubt you loved this lover dear,
And for his fate shed many a tear;
But when love's visions swift retreat,
Why cling to hope barred by defeat?
I give to you my heart and hand;
I place myself at your command;
I hold to you both wealth and fame,
And give to you an honored name;
I give to you a lovely home
Excelled by none 'neath heaven's dome.

7

This happy home of which I speak
Is one a fairy well might seek.
It stands within a lovely spot,
Where bloom the sweet forget-me-not
And roses red as sunset sky
That kiss the breezes passing by.
Close by the gate a laughing stream,
Whose rippling waters all day seem
To sport and play in merry glee,
Flows onward, onward to the sea;
Upon its banks a mountain high
Its head lifts in ethereal sky,
At whose broad base sweet flowers dwell
That always coming spring-time tell.
In such a happy home as this
Life would be but a field of bliss,

O'er which from morn to night we'd rove,
And pluck the flowers of wedded love.
I know you loved the other one
In happy days which now have gone;
But since he's gone, you only will
That you should love his mem'ry still."
And thus he pleaded for his love,
To see if he her heart could move.
She looked into his dark-blue eye,
And then to him made this reply:
"I know that many days have passed
Since with my eyes I saw him last,
But I can see him in my dreams
As plain as day, to me it seems.
I long have nursed the happy thought
That he would come with honors bought

In war, and claim me as his bride
With joy and love and soldier pride.
But should I to your suit perchance
Give ear, the very circumstance
That I love him, preferred to you
If he were here, would make you view
Me as a wretch not worth your trust,
And change your love to pure disgust."
" Indeed, not so ! " he quickly said.
" I know your love has long been fed
With hopes that he would soon return,
Which made you other lovers spurn."
" It seems he tarries long," she said,
"And I 've good cause to think him dead ;
But you I 'd only wed in part—
You 'd have my hand, he 'd have my heart.

If you deem not such love a cheat,
I throw it humbly at your feet."
At last he said : " Let it be true ;
But you will wed and love me too,
When in the future you shall find
That mem'ry only calls to mind
Dead shadows gone, and only brings
You ghosts of former happy things."
"O yes," she said; "I then will you
As freely love, and be as true
As any woman's heart can be,
If him I lose, by fate's decree,
Whom first I loved. Then be content;
Although my love is well-nigh spent,
I will reclaim enough to give
You joy and peace while you may live.

I fear he's dead, but I will wait,
To see if he through yonder gate
Shall come again at close of day
To while the ev'ning hours away.
And when the buds are on the trees,
And fragrant fumes float on the breeze
Which tell of merry, gladsome May,
If he comes not, but stays away,
I'll wed to you my hand and heart,
And peace and love which shall not part."
When thus she spoke his joy was wild,
And with a lover's joy he smiled
A smile of love, like that of Jove's
When through the sweet Olympic groves
He first obeyed love's stern behest,
And folded Juno to his breast,

Then with his godly face upturned,
That moment worlds and planets spurned
As worthless things within his sight—
Such was his joy, such his delight.
I hold that chains which anchors bind
To ships tossed by the driving wind
Would sooner from their places move
Than that bright golden cord of love
Which lives between two hearts, and holds
Them firmly bound in tightening folds.
And what is love? Let him who can
The sunlight weigh and systems scan,
Or say why worlds at different pace
Go whirling through eternal space,
Why yonder planets ever run
Their lonesome courses round the sun,

Or why the roses from the earth
Burst forth to life from secret birth,
Or tell why shafts of lightning fly
With marv'lous swiftness through the sky,
May view this world and that above,
Then tell us what we mean by love.

Chapter VIII.

AURORA from the shining east
  Herself from slumbers had released,
And with her golden fingers bright
Had torn away the veil of night,
Through which the proud, resplendent sun
Burst forth his daily course to run.
'T is spring: the drops of golden dew
Bedeck the grass with em'rald hue,
And scintillate the golden rays
Of sparkling light ten thousand ways.
Sweet roses tipped with red and green
In every waving field are seen,

And myriad birds and insects sing
To tell of merry-making spring.
The large magnolias, spotless white—
Whose hollow tubes contain some sprite
Or woodland fay—are waving high
As gayly winds go frisking by.
This is the South, now all aglow
With an enchanting floral show—
The very paradise of earth,
Where loveliness first had its birth.
The sun with scintillating rays
O'er many a field of verdure plays,
And on the field of waving green
Spreads out a golden shimmering sheen;
The soft beams kiss the lilies here,
And linger on the roses there.

It is within the South a time
Peculiar to her lovely clime.
Her noble women—shall I dare
E'en with my pen to touch the fair
And lovely creatures of this land,
Where nature with a willing hand
Has given a clime which powers possess
To range their cheeks with loveliness
Such as no Oriental dame
Can proudly boast or justly claim?
Rosetta's love, who went away
To war, still lingers; and to-day
Upon her father's large estate
There are the fair, the brave, the great,
Who drink and feast, and all rejoice
To see her wed in love her choice;

For none of them know that her heart
Has wounded been by sorrow's dart.
Four lovely maids—all Southern girls—
With hair profuse in waving curls
O'er snowy shoulders falling down,
Some auburn-gold, some black, some brown,
Are weaving garlands for the hair
Of her who is the bride.   And there
Are others too, as sweet as they
Who weave the flowers, dressed as gay
As butterflies; and they are now,
In flowing robes as white as snow,
Close by her side as loving friends
Who feel the honor she extends
To them as waiting-maids in this
Her introduction to the bliss

Of married life.   This lovely throng
Of female beauty moves along
Into a fine and spacious room
Where wait the minister and groom .
With other guests who kindly lend
On this occasion to their friend
Their presence; they congratulate
Him on the joys which him await.
The groom advances to the side
Of her his love, of her his bride,
And takes in his her soft white hand;
Those seated round now upward stand;
The sacred preacher humbly kneels,
And to the God of heaven appeals
A prayer of faith, "that he will guide
Upon the surging restless tide

Of life this bark, so soon to sail
Among the tempest wind and gale;
And prays that when life's golden sun
Its course of time for them has run,
They twain may find a peaceful rest
Within that haven of the blest
From whose bright sands and silver shore
Sails set toward the earth no more."
He rose again, this sacred man,
And in a rev'rent tone began:
" Wilt thou take her whose hand you hold
To love while young, to love when old?
And wilt thou always cherish her
Above all others, and prefer
Her charms and graces evermore?"
But now he stops, for in the door

There comes a poor-appareled guest—
Not finely clad like all the rest;
His face is haggard, woe-begone,
" He has no wedding-garment on."
He only paused a moment there,
Then gave one look of wild despair,
And forward rushed, o'ercome complete,
Fell prostrate at Rosetta's feet.
Unconscious lay he in that hall;
The house is now confusion all.
Rosetta's father, white with age,
But youthful now from livid rage,
Commands his servants to appear—
Some twenty strong—and offward bear
This uninvited guest away
Who had disturbed their wedding-day.

The servants, swift to do their task,
Or any thing their masters ask,
Quick seize the man—old, young, and small—
To bear him from the festive hall;
But as they bore him thus aside,
His sea-blue eyes both opened wide,
And in their pensive, vacant gaze
Rosetta saw what she in days
Gone by had loved—that heart and soul
Which held her own in sweet control.
A look of love her face o'ercast:
"My God!" she cried. "At last, at last!"
She spoke no more, but waved her hand;
The servants knew 't was some command,
And downward did the stranger lay,
And quick betook themselves away.

Yes, he had gone while they were young,
But still her memory round him clung;
And recollection oft would tell
Her of the one she loved so well.
Long years had passed, far time had sped,
And she had almost mourned him dead;
But now to-day to her he came
To pledge anew his heart and claim
Hers in return. She smoothed the hair
Upon his brow, where rugged care,
Through years of suffering, left its trace
Upon his noble, manly face.
"Struck down upon the bloody plain,
Long weeks and months I've wounded lain
But then I could not death embrace,
Till I again had seen your face.

One night I slept—I had a dream :
I thought we stood beside a stream,
And watched its sparkling waters flow
Through fields where buds and roses grow.
I thought I took a blossom there
And twined it in your raven hair,
But as to you some word I spoke,
From out my troubled sleep I woke,
To find that I was all alone—
My dream of happiness had flown.
I looked out through my window there :
The earth that moment was so fair,
Stretched out beneath the moon-lit sky,
It seemed to me I could not die.
And though I suffered much and long,
I knew the arm of God was strong ;

He strengthened me when hope had gone,
And 't was his hand that led me on."
"Yes, yes!" she cried; and on his breast
She laid her raven locks to rest,
And strives each day her heart to prove,
While through his kiss she whispers, "Love."
I hold there is a Power above,
That infidels cannot disprove,
Who operates His love unspent,
And recognizes each event
Of life.   Then why ourselves deceive
By saying that we can't believe
Because there is a mystery
Through which we mortals cannot see?
There 's mystery in every breeze
Which circulates among the trees,

And one in ev'ry bud and rose,
And ev'ry thing that lives or grows.
Look where you may, on ev'ry hill,
In ev'ry bubbling, flowing rill,
'Neath ev'ry sky, in ev'ry land,
And strangeness spreads on ev'ry hand.
Then shall we say, because this thing
Or that no explanations bring,
That all is false, and none is true,
This thing 's a fraud, and that won't do?
Nonsense! The strangeness which subsists
Beside the Cause proves there exists
The Grand Effect concealed behind,
And which the finite human mind
Can never see, no matter when
It exercise its utmost ken.

Young Hubert's love-career was done—
He simply lost, and Henry won;
Quite weary of the world, he hied
To foreign fields of war, and died—
As brave a soldier and as true
As he who e'er a saber drew.
My story 's told—I need not dwell
Upon Rosetta's joy, nor tell
The happy man that Henry 's been;
But on the desk I lay my pen,
And leave them in their happiness,
As those whom Heaven stoops to bless.

Finis.

www.ingramcontent.com/pod-product-compliance
Lightning Source LLC
Chambersburg PA
CBHW032101010726
47493CB00008B/2489